breathe

by

CD Reiss

Cover art designed by the author
ISBN: 194283313X
ISBN-13: 9781942833130

chapter one

MONICA

I'd told him no. That was my first mistake, apparently. My mistakes had piled up after that. He stood behind me as the sounds of the gardeners working on our lawn came through the window. Hum, *brrt*, clip. I could see them below me, between my starfish hands. I knew the window had been treated so no one could see inside in the daytime. I knew my naked body was protected from their sight, but I was naked with my hands on the glass, bent over, my feet apart, and I could see them.

"I had a meeting," I groaned. I'd groaned it a hundred times already, but he hadn't wanted any excuses or reasons why the meeting was more important than a lunch with him. I'd explain when he asked for an explanation. No sooner.

"You're a slave to this phone," he said from behind me. He was in a suit and tie. He'd made no move to undress. Not a stitch. He was completely unpredictable when he didn't want to get off or when "getting off" meant "dominating the fuck out of Monica."

"Yes, sir," I said.

He was standing out of reach, I could tell from the distance of his voice, but he might as well have been sucking me dry. And he knew it.

"This meeting." He stepped forward, his dress shoes *tiptapping* on the hardwood. "I hope it was productive."

"It was."

He didn't touch me as he came around me and leaned on the window. He held my phone up to my face. "Don't move your hands. Put the code in."

I looked up at him. The blue sky of Los Angeles stretched behind him with buttons of clouds sewn into the afternoon. He'd started cutting his copper hair shorter and letting his ginger beard grow in for a week before trimming it. He was slim and taut in his custom suit, a creature built for the vicious hunt. The cruel fuck. The tender caress in the night.

My thighs shuddered when I looked in his eyes and saw the power seated in his brutality and compassion.

"The code, Monica."

This was the brutal side.

I pressed the code into the glass with my nose, and the phone clicked open. I looked at him as he fiddled with it.

"We had a lunch scheduled," he said.

"I know, sir."

"Would you like to explain why you cancelled?"

"My new agent—"

"Maura Conrad, yes, I know her."

"She got me a gig."

"That's her job. So?"

"Singing the national anthem on opening day."

He looked up from the phone. "Really?"

"Dodger Stadium."

He smiled, stern demeanor gone. "Of course. If you sang in Anaheim, I'd welt you."

He tapped the glass, and the phone vibrated in his hand. I stiffened. He tsked.

"It's not a call, goddess."

"Yes, sir."

He got behind me and stroked my back, pressing my lower spine down and forcing my ass up. Then he put the flat glass of the vibrating phone against my skin.

"You're forgiven, of course," he said. "So consider this a reward, not a punishment."

He moved the phone across my ass and between my legs.

"Quiet now," he said, pressing it against my clit. "They can't see you, but if you scream, they'll look up here."

I didn't know how he got the phone to vibrate without a call, and constantly, for the two minutes it took for me to come silently, rising up on my toes and exposing my throat the Los Angeles sky.

chapter two

MONICA

Mrs. Yuan paused. Or to be more accurate, she didn't say anything. Shiny black chopsticks held a straw nest and a little blue bird held to the knot on top of her head, and the fact that she wasn't saying anything made me feel as though I didn't belong anywhere in her presence. Debbie had said Mrs. Yuan was the best voice coach in Los Angeles, and everyone from my new agent to the execs at the record label agreed. She was the Queen of the Vocal Cords.

I cleared my throat. Breathed. The huge warehouse windows had been closed against the street noise so she could hear me sing, and now I wanted to open them and jump to my death.

The girl at the piano didn't speak either. She just stared at her fingertips on the keys, silken black hair hanging to her forearms as if she couldn't bear what had just happened.

"What was that?" Mrs. Yuan asked, stepping forward in her red silk wrap, mandarin collar stiff against her throat.

"The 'Star-Spangled Banner,'" I said, trying to not stare at the bird.

"I thought that song couldn't get any uglier. Congratulations. You're a rare person to prove me wrong."

My skin stayed the same size. My body didn't change on the outside. But inside, I shrank into a shriveled line of brittle glass. Normally, I didn't care what anyone thought—I was too busy working my ass off. No one ever had anything bad to say about my skill anyway. Not since high school had anyone really pointed at the cracks in my technique and jabbed them.

I didn't know what to say. I could have been defensive, but I didn't feel defensive. I felt pretty sure that not only was she right, but I'd known she was right all along.

She glided over to the piano and opened a little box that had been sitting on the music rack. "I can hear your talent. Not your craft, unfortunately. I'm not quite sure I can teach you to sing in two weeks."

"I don't need to learn to *sing* per se."

"Singing isn't the problem. You barely know how to breathe."

"I just need help with the one song." Actually, I didn't need help with shit. I needed to leave and just coast on what I had for the rest of my life.

"You're breathing too late and too shallow. And you're yelling. You're so sharp you're going to draw blood."

I swallowed. She was right. I was too sharp, and I always worked around timing breaths. I'd been proud of finding a method to get around doing it right. Maybe I shouldn't have been so pleased with myself.

"Have you ever used a tuning fork?" She held the box open in front of me. Tucked inside the velvet lining sat a silver two-pronged fork with a little ball at the bottom of the handle.

"To tune my viola. But if you can't help me by opening day, I can just go." I reached for my bag.

"You paid for this session. You might as well stay."

She stood with her hands caressing the box, posture perfect, unrefusable. If Debbie found out I hadn't made it through one hour, I'd be embarrassed. I could make excuses about scheduling for every other session, but I was here now. I put my bag down, and Mrs. Yuan nodded ever so slightly. I felt as if I'd lost a chance to save myself.

"You used the fork for the viola. And your voice? You tuned with what?"

"A sharp. On the piano." I indicated the flawless black grand Steinway in the center of the room as if I had to tell her what a piano was.

"You tune your instrument to something impure, and what you get is an impure tune. They say in data analysis, garbage in, garbage out."

"The pianos were always in tune," I said defensively. "I was always careful."

She tapped the fork against a corner of the piano that was dented and bare of gloss. "This is A four forty."

"I know."

"You're so busy talking, I could be at middle C and you wouldn't even hear it."

I shut my trap. If this was how it was going to go, I'd just endure it. "Yes, ma'am," I said without a lick of snot in my tone.

"Sherri," Mrs. Yuan said.

The girl at the piano looked up.

"Give me an A please."

Sherri hit the key. Mrs. Yuan tapped the fork and put the stem to my ear.

When it quieted, she said, "Do you hear that?"

"Hear what?"

"The oscillations between the fork's tone and the piano's."

Maybe? Maybe something? They'd been the same note, but maybe...

"Can I hear it again?"

They did it again, and I listened. I knew what unmatched tones sounded like, but this was so slight, I didn't think it really existed.

"I think so?"

She tapped the fork again, and Sherri played the note again.

"I think I—"

"There is no question of it," she said, stopping the vibration with her hand. "Give me A in B octave." She tapped the fork and put the handle by my ear.

I sang a long note, matching the tone. I listened for the oscillations and heard none. The fork's note drifted to nothing, leaving me singing the note. I sounded perfect. Exactly the same.

"Make it stop," Mrs. Yuan said, throwing up her hands. "There are tire skids on the street that got closer to a pure note than you. And your breath. If you sang the whole song in A, you might not be so offensive. But the song goes from C to G to a series of flats…if your first note isn't perfect and you're panting like a Great Dane, you're a fool in front of how many?"

Was I supposed to answer? How many seats did Dodger Stadium have? I knew this by heart, but I'd emptied myself so thoroughly to survive our conversation that I'd forgotten to think.

She waited, placing the fork in the box.

"Fifty thousand something?" I sounded as incompetent as I felt.

"Something? Fifty-five thousand six hundred ninety-four. Accuracy. Accuracy and precision. This is what you need." She snapped the box closed. "There will be no charge for this session. If you want to commit to getting yourself in shape for this performance, come back tomorrow."

She spun on her heel and glided to a door. Sherri didn't make a sound as she got up, closed the lid over the keys, and followed.

chapter three.

MONICA

I didn't cry when I left Mrs. Yuan's Music School for Masochists and Fucking Morons. I got in my little Jaguar and went home without thinking about anything. All I did was pull into the driveway, go up to the bathroom, and take a shower as if I could wash the shame off me.

I sang in that little wet glass room. The vibrations bounced off the tile and water droplets, making a mess of the sound and masking everything but the emotion.

I was good enough for my label, my new agent, my fans, everyone but Mrs. Yuan. I didn't know if I'd have to send her my regrets, but I wouldn't. I just wouldn't call, period. Having made that decision, I finished up my serenade to the shampoo bottles and toweled off.

The phone rang. It was Jonathan.

"Hi," I said. "Where are you?"

"Getting on the freeway." He was in Van Nuys of all places, setting up an art foundation satellite site. He'd gotten the LA Phil to train underprivileged kids how to play stringed instruments, and I was supposed to be there.

"I should have come with you," I said, putting him on speaker.

"I know."

I'd stayed home to train with Mrs. Yuan, and he hadn't been happy about it. He thought my voice was perfect, even for the brutal 'Star-Spangled Banner' in front of fifty-five thousand whatever whatever people.

"How did your lesson go?" he asked, bringing up the exact point of our contention.

"Fine. I don't think I'm going again. I don't need it, really. Anyone can sing the 'Star-Spangled Banner.' Roseanne did it, and she didn't have any voice coaching."

"You said you were struggling with it."

"Yeah, but I feel all right now." I whipped the towel off my head and fluffed my hair.

Who was I kidding? And why was I lying about it? I was standing in front of a mirror and lying to my naked body.

"She must be really good if you got so confident in an hour."

I heard him shuffling papers around. He'd be in the back of the Bentley with Lil driving.

"Yeah, well." I opened my makeup bag. "I guess she did."

"We have two weeks. Francis Scott Key could write an anthem to what I can do to your body in two weeks. How about Hawaii?"

"I don't think I can," I said, dragging the mascara stick over my lashes. "I don't want to be jet-lagged in front of 55,695 people."

"Right. Opening day always sells out."

"You'll make it, right? You'll come?"

"Yes. And so will you. You're in the bathroom. I can tell from the echo."

"It's a really big bathroom. And marble." I rummaged through my makeup. I didn't feel like putting it on, but I was "seen" more and more often, and I hated looking like a ragmop in magazines.

"You wearing anything?"

"Nada. But I don't have time to—"

"Bend over the vanity."

"Honey—"

"Get your tits on the marble, Monica."

He couldn't see me. I could say I did it and finish my makeup. I could do a lot of things, but he needed my trust. We never photographed each other in any kind of compromising position, because we assumed at some point we'd be hacked or the pictures would leak. So it was all trust.

I bent over the vanity. It was cold and hard on my nipples.

"Ass up," he said.

I did it, and the posture alone made me wet. The exposure and vulnerability brought on a rush of need. "Yes, sir."

Tell me to touch myself tell me to touch myself tell me to

"Touch yourself."

I exhaled and drew my hand down between my legs.

"You wet?"

"Yes," I groaned.

"That's my girl. Two fingers, all the way in. Leave the clit alone. We'll get to that."

Perfect. His voice was perfect, his commands were perfect, he was—

My phone buzzed. On the marble counter, it shifted a good quarter inch from the rattle of the vibration. I peeked at the screen.

It was Mrs. Yuan.

"Jonathan?"

"Yes?"

The phone buzzed again.

"I have a call." I was surprised by how excited I was. I wasn't going to see her again, but I couldn't ignore her. I wanted her to want me. "I have to take it."

He paused, and the phone buzzed. Shit. I was going to lose her call. I got up from my position and stared at the phone as if that would get Jonathan to acknowledge it faster.

"Jon—"

"You'll be naked and on your knees when I get back. You understand?"

"Yes, okay."

"Yes, what?"

"Yes, sir."

He hung up, and I answered the call just in time.

"Mrs. Yuan?"

"Mrs. Faulkner? It's Sherri."

"Oh, hi."

Why was I disappointed? Obviously, I'd expected Mrs. Yuan to call and tell me she was wrong. I had talent. I had promise. I could find a pure note, and she still wanted to work with me despite the fact that I didn't actually need her.

"You left your sheet music here," Sherri said.

"The 'Star-Spangled Banner'? Keep it."

"It has a phone number on it?"

Damn. That was the number for Gary, the pregame coordinator. I could have gotten it again from Maura, and looked like a complete incompetent, but I was drawn to a question I needed answered.

I inhaled, pressed my lips together, then let the question out anyway. "Is she like that with everyone?"

"Like what?"

Like *what*?

What was I asking? Was she always so honest? Was she always so accurate? Or was the better question, was Monica always such a fucking baby?

"I'll come by tomorrow."

"I'll leave it on the piano."

She hung up. I'd been fine until then. I'd taken the whole episode with Mrs. Yuan in stride. Shit. She had a bird in her hair. She probably couldn't teach me.

But when Sherri hung up, it just cracked me. By being so businesslike, so factual, so careless, she had forced me to stop seeing myself how others saw me and start looking at what was really there.

And I was not happy.

chapter four

MONICA

"Take your clothes off," he said, standing in the middle of the bedroom in his suit.

He'd just gotten back and had a bottle of Perrier and two glasses sent up. I'd spent the intervening forty-five minutes trying to find my way around the "Star-Spangled Banner."

I'd discovered just how much I needed help.

"Okay," I said, yanking at my long dress, "but—"

He took a step forward and grabbed the back of my hair before I'd hit the vowel.

"Not a word," he growled in my ear. "I know your schedule better than you do."

Fluid rushed between my legs. It was almost painful, the speed of my body's reaction to the way he showed me that he didn't care on one hand, and made me feel safe in his respect of my work in the other. He wouldn't jeopardize anything important to me to fuck me. But he would fuck me.

"Yes," I said, intentionally leaving off a word.

"Yes?"

"Yes, sir."

He knew what it did to me to verbally submit. My God, we hadn't even started and I was losing myself in it.

He let go of my hair and stepped back. "Again. Take your clothes off."

He sat on the couch and watched as I stripped down quickly and efficiently. No seduction. No sway of the hips. Just me obeying him. That was the way it went down.

As I pulled off my socks, he tapped his finger on the arm of the couch, and I admired the angle of his jaw against the long perfection of his neck.

"Leave the underpants on." He said it as if he was bored, but he had a tidy erection under his suit pants. I wanted to put it in my mouth.

I stood there, perfectly still, watching him. He took his time opening the Perrier, placing the cap on the table. Pouring it. Letting the carbonation settle. Pouring more. Putting the bottle down. Picking up the glass. Sipping. The ice clicked.

"On the bed," he said, almost as an afterthought. "On your knees. Hands on the footboard. That ass better be up, or you won't be able to sit down at dinner tonight."

I got on the bed. He watched me. Everywhere his eyes landed felt exposed, vulnerable, alive. My nipples stood on end and he hadn't even touched me, and from that raw place, everything spilled out. I sniffed. Swallowed. Tried to hold my shit together, but I knew if I clammed up, he'd see it. In the quarter note's time it took me to try to clamp down on the tears and fail, my eyes filled and my lips made that horrible weeping grimace.

"I'm sorry," I managed to spit out. I had no choice but to surrender to it.

"Monica, what—?"

"It's not you." I gripped the footboard railing, ass not up, legs barely spread. I wanted him to correct me, to push me into place. Turn chaos into order.

He sat on the edge of the bed and put one hand on my back and the other on my face, pulling me toward him.

"No," I spit, my chest heaving with hitched breaths. "Just do it. Finish. I want it hard, and I want it to hurt."

"I will not."

"I need it. Please. Whatever you had planned." I couldn't see him clearly through the tears, couldn't read his face or intentions. "I need…" Breath. Hitch. Breath. "I need to get out of my own head."

"About what?"

About what? My incompetence and lack of talent. My play at being something I wasn't. If I told him what was going on, he'd try to support me and say nice things. And I didn't want that, because it was all lies. Even if he, in his ignorance, believed them, they were lies I'd told that he was repeating back to me.

"Monica, what is it?"

"Jesus fuck, Jonathan. Do it. Do something! I'm on my knees already!"

He stood. "I'm sorry, goddess. It doesn't work like that."

I got up on my knees. "What the fuck do you mean it doesn't work like that? How is it supposed to work?"

"It's not safe."

I didn't know what I'd expected him to say. I didn't know what he could have said that would have adequately soothed my loneliness. But he knew damn well *he* was safe, so what he was saying was that I wasn't safe. Not only was I a lying faker conwoman, I was somehow a danger to him. Or I was doing it wrong.

No, that was it. That fit. I was doing it wrong. I didn't know how to sub to the only Master I'd ever known. I was shitty at submitting. Shitty at fucking. I was going to get someone hurt.

Right? Wasn't that exactly it? What was I good at? Where was my core competence if I couldn't even please my husband? Not just please him, but *submit.* Meaning *do nothing.* I couldn't even sit still correctly.

I couldn't take it. My own head betrayed me. I was going to have a complete nuclear meltdown, sitting on a bed naked, because my husband wouldn't fuck me.

"Monica," Jonathan said from the next galaxy over, reaching light years to brush my cheek. "It's because—"

"Stop talking." I think I growled it before I slapped his hand off me. "And don't touch me."

I hopped off the bed. I think he was talking, but I couldn't hear shit past the *whoosh* in my ears and the yacking in my head about how he didn't want me, and how I couldn't sing, and it was all over. I wasn't a singer. I wasn't a goddess. I was a failure. A fraud. A waste.

I pulled my dress on as if I wanted to rip it apart, and I jammed my feet in my shoes.

Jonathan caught my arm at the door. "Where are you going?"

I didn't want his hand on my arm. It was the source of all my rawness. That hand. Not his soft eyes or his gentle look of compassion. No, all that was a lie. It was pity. I was beneath him, and he felt sorry for me. Fuck him.

When I glared at him, he lightened his grip, letting his fingers slip down my arm.

I had a split second of clarity.

I could fall into his arms, into his green eyes. I could break down without a beating and a fucking and just tell him how worthless and shitty I felt. I had a classic case of the Freudian Slips. Gabby's term.

And I got mad at myself again, because I'd also failed to take care of her when she needed me. The clarity went out the window.

"Monica, what is it? Talk to me. Sit down and tell me—"

He let go of me to gesture to the tea table, a comfortable place to sit and dump all my shit on him. I took the opportunity to not talk about anything.

chapter five

JONATHAN

She just walked out. She even closed the door.

I was torn between the desire to wrestle her down and demand an explanation and the need to just let her walk out so she could cool off. I didn't know which I wanted and I didn't know which she needed.

She was in the car before I decided none of that mattered and I had to get her. And it was too late. She screeched out of the driveway and down the hill, and I was left there wondering what the fuck had happened.

All right.

Well.

I knew what had happened.

I'd scared myself.

Sadism is confusing if you're not a sadist. And if you are, and your personal battle with decency is won or lost in a moment of indulgence, it's beyond confusing. It's a war between ten equally-matched nation-states who are willing to fight to the death.

She had been on the bed, naked, on her knees, and ready for me to inflict whatever the fuck I wanted on her. And I was ready. I had a plan or five. I had a boner that was breaking my zipper. I was going to rip her apart until she screamed and cried.

Fuck. She'd been gone ten minutes, I'd paced the floor for nine and a half of them, and the thought of the way she'd looked gave me an erection all over again, because I knew what I had intended to do to her. How I was going to break her.

I had to draw out the pain and tears. I had to bring her to the brink and hurt her as she tipped. The process went from A to B to C, and she'd skipped steps. Crying ahead of cue did two things.

Three things….four…ten—who the fuck even knew how many—factions went to war in my head.

I pulled the chair away from my desk so hard it went across the room, and I snapped up a pencil.

One. You cry when I say, not sooner.
Two. I can hurt you. Your defenses are down. I can go in and really fucking hurt you.
Three. I'm concerned about you. Very concerned.
Four. I want to kill whoever made you cry.
Five. You don't call the shots.
Six. I wanted to reach into your injured places and destroy you.
Seven. My heart breaks when I see tears on your face.
Eight. What kind of man thinks, "I wonder how far I can take this?"

Nine. Ten. Eleven. They were all the same. She was hurt, and I was concerned and broken, and my dick was the first thing I thought of. I hated myself for it. I wasn't an emotional sadist, but maybe I was on some level. I pressed my hands to my desk, pencil still woven between my thumb and first finger.

I had to get past the self-loathing. There was nothing there for me. Monica had taught me that I didn't have to hate myself for what made me happy. My proclivities didn't keep me from having something real and permanent, unless I let her walk away when she was hurt.

I circled number three. That was where my love was. The rest was fleeting and I'd dealt with it already. I wouldn't let her go over a little slip.

I slipped the pencil down, and my mind put together four and six.

Four. I want to kill whoever made you cry.

Six. I want to reach into your injured places and destroy you.

Maybe I was the masochist.

chapter six

MONICA

I was mad. Just steaming mad with little black lines and gritted teeth. I was foot-stomping, fist-clenching, spitting mad.

He always had to call the fucking shots. Safe. Out. Foul. He was umpire, batter, and pitcher. And fuck him. Maybe for once he should take his stinking ego and put it like...over there. Outside the bedroom. Leave it in the driveway or in the trunk of that ridiculously expensive car, because it was getting in the way of my motherfucking needs.

"I'm not mad at him," I lied to Yvonne. She knew Jonathan was my Dominant, and it made her uncomfortable. I didn't feel like explaining, yet again, my need to get hurt. "I missed you. Stay out with me. Have the sitter stay a couple of extra hours."

"Nope," Yvonne said, her body jerking back and forth with the joystick. Her huge afro moved with her, and her gold mascara glowed in the blue light. She worked three nights a week at a shithole bar on Western Ave that only took cash and gave change in quarters. The walls were lined with eighties video games at fifty cents a pop. Her shift had just ended, and she was getting loose on Galaga.

"It's on me."

"Ian's coming over once I confirm my son's asleep. And I pay my own sitter."

"I wasn't trying to insult you. And who's Ian?" I felt out of touch. She'd mentioned the name as if I should know, and I didn't. Too much travel. Too much work.

"He's the real thing."

"You didn't tell me."

Her spaceship exploded, and she whacked the red ball of the joystick. "I haven't seen you in three months unless you're on *TMZ* or something. So first you tell me what's eating you, and I'll tell you who's eating me." She waggled her brows.

How was I supposed to explain this? *I'm so fucking mad at him because I feel rejected and stupid and fake and Jonathan didn't hurt me when I asked him to. Breaking me is his responsibility as a husband and he refused and it is not cool.*

That wasn't going to fly.

Her spaceship regenerated, and she was back at the game, her dark skin shining blue from the screen.

"Nothing," I said. "Maybe hormones."

"Girl, you got a face from here to Jerusalem, and it's got Jonathan spray-painted all over it."

"You're not even looking at me."

"I got peripheral vision for this shit." She held two fingers in a V and pointed them at me with one hand while her other hand worked the joystick.

The fact that she wasn't looking at me made it easier to broach the subject.

"I have needs," I said.

"Yeah." She threaded a needle between bombs, jacking the stick back and forth.

"And he's responsible for them."

"Yeah."

"And I can't sing. I don't know what's wrong with me. Star-Spangled-Fucking-Banner, and I can't find the notes."

Boom. She lost her spaceship. Game over. She slapped the console and turned to me. "Did you ever hear Whitney Houston's version? Holy hell, I get tears in my eyes."

I imagined gold mascara running down her dark-skinned cheeks.

"She eased up on the phrasing," I said defensively. "I have to do it the hard way."

She smirked. "Oh, so you're that good, huh? Hardest song in the world shouldn't be anything for Mrs. Perfectopants."

She'd nailed me. I mean, right to the matte black wall. She'd caught my ego midair and held it still so I could see it twitching in her palm.

"I'll beat you at Galaga." I changed the subject like a real pro.

"Girl, you got nothing on me."

"Right here. Right now."

"One game, then I have to go home to the boy."

Galaga was something I was perfectly comfortable losing at. I would play my heart out and take my lumps and not even care. I reached into my bag for two quarters and saw my phone in the pocket, lit up like a Christmas tree.

Jonathan.

The sight of his name was like a little empty place in my chest. I still felt rejected. I still felt like a fraud in every aspect of my life. And I was still mad, because there were so many things I couldn't bear to lose at, and he was one of them.

"You playing or what?" Yvonne asked after she'd put her money in and hit the two-player button.

"Phone's almost out of juice." I slipped it back into my bag. "Tell me about this Ian person."

"I don't want to distract you."

"Distract me. I'm going to lose anyway."

The game started with a *wheep whoop erp erp,* and my feelings of unworthiness and rage got stuffed away for later.

chapter seven

MONICA

When I got home, it was dark outside. I walked through the empty house, and found him on the back deck, reading with his feet braced on the table in front of him and his sleeves rolled up to reveal his magnificent forearms.

"Hi," I said.

He put down his book.

"I'm sorry," I continued. "I was being a baby. I trust you. You know how to keep me safe, even from what I want."

"I'm a little torn about apologizing myself. I didn't feel comfortable, but I have a responsibility to give you what you need."

"You wouldn't make me do something I wasn't comfortable with."

"Yes, I would."

"Yeah," I said ruefully.

"If you told me what you were bawling about, that might help."

"It's embarrassing."

He laughed. Motherfucker. It wasn't even a chuckle but a real laugh, as if I'd told a whopper of a joke.

"What's so funny?" I asked.

"I tie you up and beat your ass raw until you beg me to fuck you. I can't even imagine what this big embarrassing thing is."

I took a deep breath and sat across from him, my knees pressed together, elbows on them as if I was trying to defend my heart by curling into a ball. "It's not embarrassing because it's embarrassing. It's embarrassing because of my reaction to it."

"Tell me how you're reacting, then tell me the thing."

I nodded, unscrambling the words in my head, tapping my fingertips together. "I'm acting like a fucking egomaniac. Like I'm perfect. Like I have this fragile shell around myself and someone comes and, like, taps on it—doesn't even break it—just threatens it the slightest bit, and I fall apart. Not just that—I asked them to come tap on it. But I didn't really want them to. I just wanted them to admire my shell and say how wonderful it was."

"I'm assuming this has to do with music?"

"Yes." I sniffed, feeling broken all over again. "Mrs. Yuan. I don't even know her first name. But she pointed out that I suck real bad. I don't think I'm perfect. But I do. I must if I run away the first time someone tells me what I already know. Like they looked at me and recognized what everyone else couldn't see. That I'm terrible. That I'm a liar. That I fooled everyone into thinking I have talent. And I started to believe my own lies, and I'm, like, goddamnit, why did I believe me? I feel—" Here was where I really started choking on my own spit. I couldn't slow the crying down long enough to finish the sentence.

Jonathan reached for me, but I pushed him away.

"I feel worthless." The last word squeaked out.

Jonathan pulled one of those monogrammed hankies out of his pocket and snapped it open. I smiled then sobbed again.

He put the hankie up to my nose. "Blow."

I laughed and cried at the same time.

"Just blow it out, Monica."

I blew. He squeezed my nose and rocked it back and forth.

"Hey!" I said, sounding as if I had a cold.

He pulled me to him by my nose. "I love you. And if I tell you you're not worthless, you won't believe me."

He took the hankie away and balled it up on the table. His lashes glowed amber in the patio light, and the mating calls of the crickets suddenly sounded sexy as hell.

"If you never sang another note, I'd still love you," he said.

"I know and—"

"Shh." He held up his hand then held mine. "That being said, your voice is what I fell in love with before I fell in love with the woman behind it."

"So you say."

"And your body. I liked that."

"Yeah, well—"

"And your moxie."

"My *moxie*? How old are you, grampa?"

His eyes glittered green with amusement, and his hands found their way between my knees. He yanked my knees open with a swiftness that made me gasp.

"Tonight, I'm going to hurt you. I'm going to make you beg for mercy. I'm going to break you down so hard so you don't have to be broken down over this bullshit. I'm the only one who gets to make you cry."

"God, yes."

"What's your safe word?"

"Tangerine."

He leaned back and crossed his ankle over his knee. After looking me over for a second, he picked up his book and opened it. "Go into the bedroom. When I get there, you'd better be ready."

chapter eight

MONICA

He made me wait.

He always made me wait when he was serious, and the longer I waited, the more serious he was. I thought, as I waited on the bed with my cheek on the bedspread and my ass in the air, that he was making me wait longer than ever. The anticipation made the backs of my legs tingle. I wanted to touch myself. At first I thought I'd just see how wet I was, but he'd know and he'd punish me by not letting me come.

He said nothing when he finally entered the room. He stood by me. I couldn't see him. I could only feel his presence, hear his breath, sense his intentions.

He laid his hand on my lower back and pressed down. It was the standard correction. My ass was never high enough.

"Thank you," I said.

He stood and undid his belt. "Thank me later. Get on your back and open your legs. Knees up. I want to see that cunt."

I did it. He positioned himself at the foot of the bed, where I could see him between my legs. Half-open shirt and cock-strained trousers. Belt looped in his right hand. Watch and wedding ring on his left.

I almost came just looking at him. When he reached over and pulled my legs apart wider, I lost myself in a rush of sensation.

"Did you just come?" he asked.

"I'm sorry."

He shook his head. "You're going to hurt for that."

"Yes, sir."

"Open your mouth." I did, and he put the belt in it.

"You know I don't do toys," he said, running his hands over the length of my inner thigh, engaging just enough nail to wake up my skin. "Toys are for children. But sometimes I have to make allowances for safety." He sat on the bed next to me and held up an oddly-shaped glass bulb about two inches long. "Do you know what this is?"

"Yes. It's a butt plug," I said around the belt, and it sounded like a series of grunts.

"I don't want to be gentle, but I don't want to harm you either. This is the solution. And I can't makeshift one out of stuff around the house because I don't want to take you to the hospital when something breaks inside you."

He took out the belt. I had enough time to lick my lips before he grabbed my cheeks, forcing my mouth open, and put the butt plug in my mouth.

"Get that wet for me."

I rolled my tongue around the slick glass. It pressed my tongue to the bottom of my mouth. I puckered my lips around the narrow part, sucking until the flat stopper pressed against my lips like a pacifier.

Jonathan went back to the foot of the bed and looped the belt back up. I held my legs open with my hands.

"Now, first. The original issue. You're mine. When you let someone else get to you, you deny me my ownership. That is not acceptable." He tapped my inner thigh with the belt. "I own you. I can get inside you. I can hurt you. I own your pain. No one else."

The first *thwack* to my inner thigh came without warning, and it was as hard as he'd ever hit me. I screamed into the glass bulb and rolled.

"On your back, Monica. Take your medicine."

I rolled back and gingerly spread my legs. He whacked the other side. I screamed again, and tears rolled down my face.

He waited, ever patient, until I got back to center. He yanked my legs apart. "Don't roll again. You stay on your back, and you show me what's mine—only mine—to hurt."

I spread my knees, biting the thin part of the plug. The places he'd whacked still stung. Even when he put two fingers inside me, the pain didn't go away. It just moved up a level to a layer of pleasure, and I groaned into the plug when he twisted his fingers inside me.

"You're fucking soaked."

He ran his fingers over my clit twice, and I almost came again.

"Oh no, goddess. You still need to be punished for that."

He stepped back, and I braced myself for what was to come. His face was deep in concentration and arousal, lids hooded, lips apart slightly. His pleasure was mine as much as mine was his.

On that realization, he pulled his arm back and rained three strikes on my left thigh. When I screamed and twisted, he pulled me back, spreading my legs and giving me three on the right.

I couldn't see him through my tears. He pulled the plug out of my mouth, leaving a trail of cry-spit between us. He made nothing of my sobbing. He owned it. If he didn't want me to cry, I wouldn't be crying.

"Open your ass for me."

I put my hands over my ass and pulled the cheeks apart. He pulled me open with his fingers, looked at what he had to work with, and pressed the plug against my ass.

"How you doing, goddess?"

"Okay," I sobbed.

"Do you remember your safe word?" He pushed in the plug. It was wider than it looked, and my asshole stretched.

"Ah! Hurts!"

"Safe word?"

"Tangerine and fuck you."

"Breathe, brat," he said, jamming it in. He pulled it out so the widest part stretched me.

I breathed, and he stroked my clit slowly then kissed it. My body relaxed when his lips touched me, and when his tongue flicked my clit, my back arched with pleasure.

The plug slid in and stayed.

"Legs down. Get on all fours. Let me see."

When I pressed my legs together, I felt the welts. They were shockingly painful, yet I felt a rush of happiness and well-being when they stung.

Behind me, I heard the rustle of clothing. He was getting naked. Bless him. Bless him, bless him, he was going to fuck me. I closed my eyes and let the wash of contentment run through my veins.

He ran his hands through my hair, grabbed a fistful, and twisted my head toward him. He looked at my face, as if checking on me. Satisfied, he got a knee on the bed.

"Open your mouth. It gets fucked first."

I opened up. I had no choice. I wanted nothing more than his cock in my throat, and I took it. All of it, looking up at him. He pushed all the way down, pumping my face five times before pulling out so I could breathe.

"Safe word? You got it?"

"I know it," I said then opened my mouth for him.

He gripped my hair hard. "Good."

He shoved my face onto his cock and fucked my throat, pulled away long enough for me to breathe or safe out, then fucked my mouth again. I was panting when he finally stopped.

"Good girl. Would you like to come?"

"Yes, please."

"I'm going to punish you for the first time you came. Are you ready?"

"Yes."

He pushed me onto my back and opened my legs. He slid his hand between them, rubbing me with four fingers, then he slid them inside.

"Oh, God."

The next thing was a surprise. The slap right on my cunt was painful and sharp, making me scream. It blossomed into a hint of pleasure.

"You get three. That was one. Count." He slapped it.

"Two."

Again, and hard.

My back arched, and I cried out. "Three!"

"You're so fucking good," he growled, moving his hands over me. "Look at me. I love you. Come now."

I didn't answer. I couldn't. Not when he stroked me like that. I'd been bursting before he even touched me, so on his third stroke, my ass clenched and the pain of the welts disappeared as I came into his hand.

I came off the high when he pulled the plug out of my ass. I gasped.

He reached for his night table drawer and got out a washcloth and lubricant. The plug went into the washcloth, and the lube went all over my ass. I put my hands in his hair and turned to my side. He got up on his knees and put my right leg over his right shoulder.

"You ready?" he asked.

"Yes, please. Do it hard. Make it hurt."

He did, thrusting his huge cock into my ass in two strokes. It stretched me to the point of pain just the way I liked, but the pain didn't have the same sharpness I felt when he fucked it without a plug. I was full. Too full. Breaking softly around his cock.

"How is that?" he asked, leaning over my bent leg to kiss my cheek.

"Fuck. So good. So fucking…my God."

His hips moved faster, deeper, pushing into my ass. He flicked my clit, and even though I'd just come, the rising tide of another orgasm filled me.

He put his face to my cheek and owned me, breathing hard in my ear. His right arm was looped under my right leg, and he flicked my clit. Not one part of my body wasn't aware of his presence.

I owned him. I made this beautiful man gasp in my ear. His pleasure was mine, and my pain was his.

"Hurt me, Jonathan. Hurt—"

He pinched my clit, and I screamed. Pain drove through me, and the orgasm was so powerful, such a braid of sensation from both ends of the spectrum, that I nearly lost consciousness. My ass clenched, pulsing around him.

"Yes. That." He grunted and thrust deep, then stilled in his release.

When he took the last gasp, I rolled onto my back, and he slid his dick out of me.

"You're amazing," he said, kissing my face. His cheeks were rough, and I enjoyed the scratchy sensation. "Literally. You amaze me. How good you are."

"I love you."

"I adore you." One last peck on the lips, and he stood, holding out his hand. "Let me take care of you."

***

After the shower, he sat me on the cold marble vanity and had me spread my legs with my heels on the edge of the counter. The welts inside my thighs were an angry red, and looking at them made me want to get fucked again.

"I did a number on you," Jonathan said, rubbing a soothing cream over them. His touch was firm and gentle, healing and arousing.

"I needed it."

"You going back for coaching?"

"No," I said. "I think I burned that bridge. I can just practice. I'll get it."

He slid two fingers inside me, and I pushed into them.

"You'll get it."

"Oh, say can you see…" I groaned.

"I was saving your cunt for last."

"Take it."

He carried me into the bedroom and made love to me, healed me, brought me back to center. No one could hurt me with this man at my side.

chapter nine

MONICA

If you're told you're fantastic enough times, you start to believe it. And it was becoming a problem. I was at a plateau. I'd found where I belonged and was getting recognition from people with the power to make my dreams happen. It was their job to make sure I was happy and satisfied so that I'd continue working.

Unfortunately, they were businesspeople. They weren't artists or fans. They didn't know shit.

I could sing like the sound of a car screeching on asphalt, and it didn't matter to them as long as I made money. "Sell it, don't smell it" was the rule on the western end of Wilshire. And because I'd been traveling around with Jonathan, no one criticized me. My artist friends were back in LA, and I was too busy to just sit around making work with them. No one told me where I could be better. It was ass kissing time all the time.

Truth be told, I was really happy coasting. But the thing about coasting is that at some point, the energy goes out of the work, and I would have to push or grind to a halt.

"Should I wait?" Lil called back to me as she pulled me up to Mrs. Yuan's warehouse in Boyle Heights.

"Yeah. I'll be a second."

She put the car in park right in the red zone and opened the back door for me.

"You probably don't even have to turn the car off."

I could have sent her up for the music. I could have stayed home even, and sent her while I worked on the national anthem in the privacy of my home studio. But I went myself for reasons I couldn't even tell myself. I wanted to touch where the pain of the day before had been.

Yep. Pain. On the elevator, I admitted to myself that I'd been hurt, and I'd been hurt because I surrounded myself with businesspeople who didn't know how to be critical. I hadn't sat in a studio with a producer and had my ass beaten in two months. I'd gotten soft, and I bruised easily.

The door to the big white room with the black grand piano was open. I walked in, my shoes echoing. No one was there, but my stupid sheet music was on the piano.

Behind the door Mrs. Yuan had walked out of, I heard the *snipsnap* of an Asian language.

And on the lid over the keys was the black box.

I put the music back and opened the box.

A tuning fork isn't an expensive item, but it was nestled inside velvet as if it were a jewel. I tapped the worn ridge of the piano and listened to the hum of A four forty.

Singing the note wasn't something I decided consciously; it was something I did out of compulsion. I had to mimic it. Had to try it again. I couldn't just let the vibrations hover in the air without matching them.

I put the bar to my ear and sang it low at first, listening for the wave oscillations I could pick out with stunning accuracy on the viola.

I heard nothing.

I tapped the fork again and committed to doing this stupid, pointless thing. I wasn't trying to prove I could, or that I wasn't as bad as she thought. I wasn't trying to get it right even. I was trying to hear what she heard.

I sang louder. Maybe that was the issue. Maybe I just needed to sing louder to hear it.

Could have been I was screaming, or singing loud enough for Disney Hall. When the inner door snapped open, my sudden silence fell like an anvil over the room.

Mrs. Yuan stood in the doorway in a pale blue wrap. The chopsticks in her hair had little fans on them, and her mouth was a straight red slash. "Why do you come in here to torture my ears?"

She strode into the room, making the seven steps in the time it took me to put the tuning fork back in the box. I snapped it closed when she held out her hand.

"You got worse. I didn't think it was possible. What did you do to your throat?"

Jonathan's dick had been down it, but I didn't say that. "Sorry."

She took the box. I grabbed my sheet music and walked out. I noticed the molding on the door was red on the white wall, which didn't matter one bit. Just a simple observation I hadn't made last time. Why hadn't I noticed?

Because the last time I walked out, I'd been looking at the floor. This time, I was looking up, and by the time my hand touched the doorknob, I knew why.

I turned before opening the door. She was halfway back to the white inner door.

"Wait," I said brazenly.

She didn't have to wait, of course, and if she didn't respect me at all, she wouldn't have.

But she did. She stopped and turned to me.

"I dreamed my whole life of singing Dodger Stadium," I said. "I grew up in Echo Park, and I could hear everything. Sometimes I dreamed I'd be a seventh inning act, God Bless America and all, and sometimes it was a whole concert, when I was feeling really ambitious. But this? I heard someone sing the national anthem eighty days a year, and they were always bad. Always. Even when they were good, between the sound system and the octave changes, the national anthem always sounds bad in a stadium. It's a capella, and it's like I'm naked. Everything's against the performer. And I can't bear the thought of not being the best. Which is why I had such a hard time yesterday."

She folded her hands in front of her, still holding the black box, tilted her head, and said nothing for too long. "Everyone is bad, then?"

"Whitney Houston," I said. "She was great. But she used weird phrasing."

"You are not Whitney Houston."

"No, I'm not."

More silence. It hung at the perfect key for a new start.

"Can I come back?" I said. "I have two weeks. It's not enough time to find perfection, but maybe I can get closer?"

She stepped forward. "You have nothing to do for two weeks but tone your voice. Nothing. You will think in scales. You will be silent unless you are singing. You will repeat repeat repeat. At home and with me to the point where your voice is tired, but not over that line."

"Yes."

"For two weeks, I own you. Is that clear?"

"Yes."

"Now." She straightened herself when I thought she couldn't get any straighter. "I have twenty-one minutes to spare. Would you like to start?"

In my gratitude and relief, I had no other answer but, "Yes."

MONICA

I bounced into the house. Jonathan was in his running gear, finishing up a puke-colored protein shake. I kissed his cheek and rinsed out the blender pitcher.

"What took you so long?" he asked.

"She gave me homework, and we set up a schedule for the week."

"So there's hope for you?"

"Apparently not, but she's martyring herself for my sake."

He pressed himself to me, pinning my hands behind me. "I'll make you sing."

"We need to talk about this for a minute."

He let me go, and I turned to him. He pressed himself against me.

"Okay," he said, picking up my shirt. Jesus, he had such a one-track mind. I tried to pull it down, but he shooed my hands away and yanked my bra up over my breasts. "Talk."

"I have to protect my throat for the next two weeks."

"Wear a scarf."

He bent down and kissed my breasts, licking the nipples until they were hard. I dug my fingers in his hair. God, he knew how to use his mouth.

"The inside," I said. "Warm tea with honey. Soothing food." He took a good, hard suck, and my back arched toward him. "Not dick." I groaned it, because I wanted the dick. I wanted it a lot.

He knelt in front of me and unbuttoned my pants. "Two weeks, no oral. You'll make it up to me."

"I can't scream either."

"Happy to gag you if you want." He wiggled down my pants.

"And crying. I can't have too much gunk in my throat."

He stopped trying to wedge me out of my clothes and looked up at me. "Anything else?"

"I see her when she has time. She owns me, she said."

"She what?"

"It's a figure of speech."

He stood, putting his finger in my face as if about to make a point. Stopped. Raised it again. Pressed his lips into a line. Looked away.

"You're not threatened by a voice coach, are you?"

That did it. Whatever indecision had been interrupting the flow of his thoughts was driven away by my pure snottiness.

"Bend over the sink. I'll show you who owns what around here."

chapter eleven

JONATHAN

I didn't know if she said someone else owned her to annoy me or to prepare me for the coming weeks, because once I'd had her over the counter, she kissed me, cleaned herself off, and started.

Scales.

All fucking day and night.

Monica's voice went straight from her throat to my higher self. Its vibrations were coded to the wavelengths of my heart.

But scales? All the fucking time? No words. No melody. Just up up up up and down down down down. Do re mi fa so la ti do without the cheerful little animals and sunshine. Or, more specifically, without a point.

"Monica?" I said, peeking into her studio.

She finished the scale. "Yeah."

"I'm going to lunch with Eddie."

"Okay."

She didn't just say okay though. She ran though half a scale to do two syllables.

I loved her. I'd give my life for her. And she looked like a queen just standing in the middle of the room with her mouth open and her hand clutching that stupid fucking fork. But, man, I would have preferred a smart-ass answer to the boring earnestness of those notes.

"There's a thing in March," I said. "In New York. It's a contest for money for the Arts Foundation. It's more for the prestige than anything. All the guys are going."

She tapped her fork and put the handle to her ear, keying, then answered. "When is it in March?"

I gritted my teeth, because she didn't ask the question. She sang "When" to *do,* "is" to *ray,* "it" to *mi,* "in" to *fa,* "Ma" to *so,* she took a second "Ma," and added "rch" to *la.* It wasn't lost on me that she would have normally asked "When in March?" but needed the extra syllables for the full scale.

"First weekend," I replied, and she tapped the fork. It vibrated. She opened her mouth to answer, but I couldn't bear it. "If you answer me in scales, I'm putting a collar on that pretty little throat."

She stood there, straight as an arrow, fork at her chest as if in prayer. I felt half an ounce of regret and a gallon or more of desire. The throat. I hadn't had my dick down it in too long. It had become a prized piece of real estate, and I was losing a bidding war.

Then, like a child testing her limits, she tapped the fork.

I thought I made it to her in two steps. I didn't know what I was thinking, but I put my hand under her chin and pressed myself against her.

"You're pushing me." I was gentle on her neck, but she couldn't move.

"I have something the first few days in March," she said.

Those were her words. And though she was telling me all kinds of truths, the words were a lie because she wasn't talking about her schedule. What she was actually saying was *I'm not scared of you.*

Which was fine. I didn't want her to be scared. I just wanted her to stop answering in vocal exercises. I wanted her to submit. Abdicate. All of it. To me. And she hadn't in a week. I'd topped her, but it hadn't been *that*. She was a china doll.

I wanted to own her again, but since she started with this teacher, she'd been distracted. Yes, I respected her talent. She needed her career and her work to thrive as a human. But I was getting frustrated, and it came out when I spoke into her cheek in the low register of a command.

"You have plenty in March. You'll be so sore you won't be able to walk. But that first weekend, you show where I tell you to show, or I take you on a leash."

Her jaw set against my fingertips, but her eyelids fell a fraction of an inch. I got my free hand under her skirt. She had garters on, and stockings that stopped an inch below her beautiful cunt. I short work of getting around her lace panties.

"You're wet. Again." I drew my fingers along the length of her wetness and back. "Was it the leash? The collar? Or knowing how I can hurt you?"

"You can hurt me after opening day." A smirk played on the edges of her lips, then she gasped when I put my fingers inside her. "Save it up," she groaned.

"I'm going to destroy you."

Two strokes, and she clenched and came, toes curling so hard her shoe fell off. But she didn't scream. She didn't say a word. I put my fingers in her cunt and felt it tighten and release, then tighten again as I rubbed her clit with the heel of my hand. She threw her head back, exposing her bare neck.

That throat. The length of it. The curves and rises no less than a topography of possession.

I let her go.

She straightened her skirt, looked at me, and tapped her fork. *Do do do. Do do re. Do do mi—*"

"What's that?" I asked, grinding my teeth at this new pattern of offense.

"Intervals. You like?" She raised an eyebrow.

I was going to respect her talent and her music. I was going to give her space. I was going to be a supportive and good partner no matter what. Another six days. But she wouldn't be finished with the word *brave* before I bent and broke her.

chapter twelve.

MONICA

Mrs. Yuan hadn't come to the club. I felt both good and bad about that. Sherri was there with a little klatch of Asian girls, but she didn't look at me. I could only assume she was there to report back.

From the stage, I saw Jonathan sitting to the side with Leanne, who was talking on her cell phone while picking at her shoe, and Maura, my new agent. Eddie was there. Darren's buddies were with his husband, Adam. Mostly though, the Thelonius Room was packed with strangers. Not fifty-five thousand of them, but scale wasn't the issue. Singing this bitch of a song in front of anyone was the issue.

Jonathan had threatened to collar me five days before. We'd always been at war over the concept, and as I learned more about it, my opinion hadn't changed. He owned me. He didn't need me to walk around in a collar to prove it. And I didn't need to feel owned in that way. A little humiliation was fine and part of the game, but a collar?

No.

Just no.

I wasn't a dog, and though I was completely submissive, I wasn't a slave.

End of.

Except....

Except when I let myself think of him pulling on it, or imagined how it would feel during the day, how it would remind me of him, or how it would feel to kneel before him and look up enough so he could see the symbol of my tender obedience.

I breathed into the bottom of my lungs, filling the widest part first, to the top, then exhaled slowly.

Darren whipped a quick beat on his drum. To my right, Harry, the bassist from Spoken Not Stirred, and Steve, the guitarist, was to my left. Evanie sat to the side, always an excellent sport when Monica Faulkner showed up to sing. It was because of Evanie that they'd gotten a deal and a little tour that would take them to Nashville right after they finished Thelonius.

They played a few notes, and the crowd quieted. I smiled. I loved that moment of expectation, anticipation. The vacuum I was meant to fill.

"You all know Monica Faulkner," Harry said, putting his hand out to me. Applause. Whistles. "She's gonna open with a classic."

"Thank you, guys," I said, looking at each of them. Darren had offered me this opportunity to work out my nervous kinks, and it had seemed like a fun idea at the time.

Still thinking this would be a fun tryout, I sang the first few words.

Oh, say can you see....

Harry popped the bass a little, but I was otherwise a capella. Then something I didn't expect happened. Everyone stood and put their hands on their hearts.

You were supposed to stand. It was a rule. But the scraping of chairs and the good-humored salutes distracted me, because in the first second, I thought they were getting up and leaving. They were a bunch of freaking hipsters after all, not the most reverent type. So I faltered. They were leaving because I'd insulted their sense of irony.

But I was wrong. They were staying.

I adjusted to that, but in doing so, I diverted precious mental bandwidth.

And my voice went off the fucking rails. A key is a bookmark. If you know where you are, you can travel up and down the scales accurately.

But I lost my place. I kept to the beat and knew the words, but the key was all screwed up. Before I even got to *ramparts,* I was fighting tears, and that was the hardest line. It led into *gallantly streaming,* which was flat as fuck, and led into *rocket's red glare,* which felt superhumanly sharp and high, and I had no way of getting there.

I got to the *home of the brave* and smiled, but I wanted to die. Oh sure, they clapped, because it was fun and unexpected and even ironic. But they didn't get what a complete fuckup that had been, and I'd almost done it in DodgerStadium.

I'd almost sounded like that in front of 55,695 people.

There were lists on YouTube of the worst game-time renditions of the "Star-Spangled Banner," and I was about to be one of them.

I had to get out of this.

I shook hands and smiled and did all the things on my way to the back room. My stuff wasn't in that room though, since I wasn't a real act. My bag was next to my husband, and I was supposed to sit by him and have a drink and plan little adjustments to my song. But there were no little adjustments. There was my quitting and staying home with a beer and a flat screen on opening night, or there was a complete overhaul I didn't have time for.

So I went into the back room where Darren had his shit, and I closed the door behind me. My hands were shaking as hard as my knees. I leaned against the makeup counter. The linoleum edge was chipped down to the wood. It looked like Mrs. Yuan's piano where she habitually hit the fork. I pressed my thumb against the ridge.

What was she going to say? She'd seemed pleased with my progress, and now what would Sherri go back and report?

I wanted to throw up.

There was a knock on the door. I knew who it was.

"Jonathan, just leave me be."

He came in carrying my bag. "You want to go out the back?"

"I want to die."

"I didn't give you permission to die." He dropped the bag on the counter.

"How bad was it?"

He shrugged. "You've sounded better. But you psyched yourself out."

"I should back out, right? Claim a sore throat?"

"No. Quitting's not your style."

Outside, Darren's band started playing loud and fast.

I stood and grabbed Jonathan's belt. "How about this?" I tapped my throat. "You fuck my face so hard I can't even speak. Really get it in there. Down the throat all the way. You'll get your dick sucked, and I'll get out of opening day."

He started laughing before I was even done. Fucker.

"I can't, Jonathan. I can't do Dodger Stadium." I pulled out his belt. "But this? Your dick? That I can do. I should have just stuck to that in the first place."

He slipped his hands over mine and pulled them off his pants. "I've been annoyed with the whole thing, I admit. But I want you to see it through. I can take being a little annoyed. I'm a big boy."

I crossed my arms and leaned my butt on the counter. I felt petulant and immature. I wanted to kick dirt and stick out my tongue.

"You can do this," he said.

"Fuck you." I pouted right through the cuss.

"Maybe you need to use the fork before you start next time."

"I hate that thing."

"Me too. Where is it?"

I pointed my chin at my bag. "Right in there. Coulda used it, but noooo…Miss Egopants didn't need it."

He plucked the box out of my purse. When I'd committed to the process, I'd gotten a little black bracelet box out of a drawer for my fork, just like Mrs. Yuan's. I wanted to be as reverent as she was. Jonathan removed the fork and tapped it.

The tines hummed.

"It's too late," I said. If he made me sing, I would seriously turn into a brat the likes of which…

He put the fork to my lower lip.

"It tickles." I slapped it away.

He put his hand on my throat and held me still, tapping the fork again. "Hush now."

His voice left no room for argument. It was a fact. I was hushing. I was submitting. I was letting him do whatever he wanted, because he was my king, and his voice let me know a king was precisely what I needed.

He put the fork to my lower lip. It tickled like mad, and I fought to stay still.

"How long is Darren's band going to play?"

"Half an hour, forty minutes."

"Lean back." He locked the door.

"You know why I failed tonight?" I said.

"Why?" He put the tuning fork in his pocket and pulled up my shirt.

"I got cocky. I practiced just enough to think I had it but not enough to get it right."

"You're really hard on yourself. I didn't know that about you." He put his hands up my skirt, simultaneously exposing me and drifting over my inner thighs. "You're either a talentless hack because you have to work on your craft, or you're a lazy ass because you don't work hard enough."

"Maybe I'm both."

He slid off my underwear. "Sure. You're a master con artist. Everyone's fooled. Why aren't your legs spread? Come on. Let's work on this position. I have something to propose."

He picked up my knees and placed my heels on the edge of the counter, then he pulled them apart until I was completely exposed to him. God, his eyes on me made the air between us into a solid mass I could rub up against.

"Shoulder blades together. Good." Gently, he put his hand under my upper back and pulled it up until my lower back was straight and my tits stuck out. "Put your head back. I want to see that throat. I want to see where the music comes from."

The top of my head brushed against the mirror. I felt thrust forward. Exposed. Vulnerable. As if I was attacking with my soft underbelly. Only trust made this possible.

"How are you doing?" he asked.

"Fine, sir."

"I want you to keep your mind between us. What note is this?"

"A."

He tapped the fork. It hummed to A, and I fought the urge to join it to see if I could match it with my legs spread. But all I was angled to see was the cracked ceiling.

The fork touched my lower lip again before he drew it down to my throat, ever so lightly, so the vibrations wouldn't stop.

"Don't answer," he said. "Let me talk."

He tapped again and put one of the tines to my nipple, and I stiffened. The sensation was so intense. He shushed me, got me back to center, and put the vibrating fork to my other nipple. The pleasure went right between my legs.

"You trust me," he said. "And I trust you. What we do, it's no one's business. But I think you lose me when you're running around chasing perfection. I think your mind wanders, and I want to bring you back to me—to us—when you need it."

Tap.

And the little tingling vibration inside my right knee and coursed upward. The flinching tension of my cunt as he got closer, a recoil couched in desire. He got six inches and tapped again. God, it tickled and sent me wild. I wanted it, and I didn't. He tapped again. Left side. Wince. Want. Gasp as he got close.

Tap. Circling the tingling vibrations along the outermost part of my lips. I squeaked.

He put his other hand on my throat, covering it. "Let me hear you."

He tapped the fork, and I hummed in A, my vocal cords safe against his hand as he touched my clit with the fork. I bucked like an animal, and he held me with the safety of his hand.

"I want to feel the note."

I stayed on A, or as close as anyone could manage with the tines of a tuning fork vibrating against her clit. He worked lightly, or the vibrations would stop, putting it lengthways against me, just enough to get me so close. So close. He tapped again when it stopped and put it against me so lightly it drove me wild.

"Don't stop," he said, tapping again. "And don't come."

"I can't I can't—"

"You can."

Again with that vibrating piece of metal on me. I was so wet that he only touched the juices flowing from me. The liquid quivered, and my humming broke into a hitch.

He tapped again.

"I can't," I said. "I can't not come."

"Keep humming. You look stunning. You sound perfect. You're going to come until you can't breathe, but not until I say."

He put it on me again. I was on fire. I existed between my legs and below my chin. If I stopped humming, I'd come, and if I came, I'd stop humming. That note, which was probably off by a lot, was the only thing keeping me from exploding.

The vibration in the fork tapered to nothing, and I prayed he wouldn't tap it again.

"Close your eyes," he said, putting the fork down. "No shouting. We don't want to strain that voice."

I did, thankful for the relief to my aching clit. He was going to let me come, he had to. I was throbbing to the breaking point.

"I only expect you to wear this in our personal space," he continued. "And I should discuss it with you, but I want you to feel it, not react to the sight of it. Do you trust me?"

I swallowed. Did I? "Yes."

I dropped the sir because he needed to know I wasn't saying it in a scene. I trusted him in all things.

He put his hand on my throat again, then behind me. I felt a tightening then a click.

"Hey." I stiffened.

He pushed me back down, putting his beautiful face close to mine, a groan escaping his lips. "This"—he ran his thumb along the edge of the collar—"is magnificent."

"Jonathan." I wanted to explain why I hated it, but I didn't have a real explanation.

He stepped back, pulled me off the counter, and turned me, putting my back to his chest.

"Look at it," he whispered in my ear.

I did as he asked. It was silver chain mail, an inch and a half wide, with a tiny lock in the front. He pushed my hair out of the way and ran his fingers over it, tugging on a ring at the back of my neck. Standing with my clothes askew and my pussy still on fire, I felt like a possession. His possession.

"I don't know."

With a slight push to my shoulders, he said, "Put your hands on the counter. I'm going to fuck you until you know."

I leaned down, and he yanked my head back by the hair.

"Look at it. Do you know what that does to me? I'm so fucking turned on right now, I'm blind. I own you. I can see how I own you. You're wearing my collar. Fuck."

He picked up my skirt. I groaned when he put his hand on my ass then slapped it hard. The pain, the arousal, and the sight of the collar put me in a place of acceptance that was lower than low and higher than high.

He undid his pants, removing that spectacular, powerful cock. I put my ass up, and he slapped it again.

"Thank you," I gasped.

He got a finger around the ring and pulled with just enough pressure to make me feel him. I must have stiffened.

"After opening day, I won't be so gentle with the ring. Now, open up for me."

He spanked me again, letting the ring go. I grabbed my ass cheeks and pulled them apart. He guided himself into my soaked pussy then slammed forward. I grunted.

"Hush," he said. "Not a sound out of you. Just take it like a good girl."

He got the rest of the way in, and my mouth opened, but nothing came out. I became nothing but a vessel for his pleasure. He moved me where he wanted me, pounding me, and I was slick and receptive.

"Look, Monica." He pulled my hair and jerked me to nearly standing. "Look at yourself." His hand went around my hips, and he wedged his fingers between my legs. "I put that collar on you. You're my property."

As he uttered it, I lost myself. Keeping my eyes open became difficult. His cock battered me, his eyes soothed me, and his collar debased me into a space so submissive, I couldn't remember my name.

"You ready to come, Monica?" he growled.

I made a little noise. My mouth was open. My eyes half closed.

"Fuck. You are so hot. Come with me. Give it to me." He slammed me. "Give me everything."

With his permission, I exploded into a soundless howl. Thighs tightening, fingers curling. He gripped my ass so tight it hurt, prolonging the orgasm with the pain, intensifying it. He thrust into me so hard I thought I'd break and all my pleasure would spill out.

He growled as if he were trying to wedge his whole body into mine. He was coming, and hard. A sound came from me as if pushed out, because I was flooded with a new warmth, a second-tier climax that burst from the inside. Soul to skin and back again.

"Oh, God," I whispered, because it wasn't stopping. "Oh god, oh god, oh god. I'm still...I'm still..."

And tears, and blackness, and the places where I was sore. After three thrusts that jerked upward as if he was making a point, he stopped. In the mirror, I saw him panting, my collar, my submission leaking away, and regular life coming back to replace it.

Jonathan ran his hands down my back then back up, gently turning me to face him. He looked barely conscious himself.

"Thank you," he said. "You're a goddess."

He said it without irony or condescension. As if he was stating a fact.

"The collar," I said.

"Yes?"

"Bedroom only?"

"To start."

Outside, the band stopped.

We reacted immediately. He got his dick in his pants, and I dropped my skirt and got my shirt arranged. He gathered the fork, the bag, whatever. Against the clatter of a pre-encore band coming down the hall, Jonathan unlocked the door. I thought nothing of it, because it should be unlocked before they got their hands on the knob.

But when it opened and the guys were right there, I realized why Darren raised his eyebrow before he said hello.

I still had the collar on.

chapter thirteen

JONATHAN

They say men and women don't communicate about their problems because women just want to feel and men just want to fix.

I'd never given that much thought.

But I wanted to fix Monica's problem with her voice, and she just wanted to go through the wringer. I was suggesting she submit her problems with her art not necessarily to me, but just in general. Overall. To do the job without worrying about what other people thought about it. She could give up this idea she was a fraud if she blocked out everyone but me, the one person who loved her whether she sang on key or not.

That made perfect sense in my head.

Also, that collar.

It elongated her neck, made her submission into an aesthetic. She became a work of art. My work of art. The sight of it put gravity-strength pressure on my balls, and when I pulled on that ring, I nearly came from seeing it in the mirror.

But when her friends entered the room, she put her hand on her throat as if that would hide it. If they knew we had been fucking, she wouldn't care. But the submission thing? That bothered her. And being collared in public was always a sticking point.

I wanted to rip the thing off before we left the dressing room, but it had a lock, and ripping something off her in front of everyone would have been quite a spectacle.

"Hi," she said, hand to throat.

They didn't even look at her. Darren murmured something. Harry said hello but was focused on getting his bass into the bag. The drummer punched my arm, and the other guy glanced at her and thanked her for opening the set.

The girl singer looked me up and down in the way women sometimes do, but their chatter was about the set, the songs, a patois of terms I didn't understand but knew had nothing to do with Monica's neckwear. She turned to me, smiled, and held out her hand.

I snapped up her bag, grabbed her hand, and walked out.

chapter fourteen

MONICA

I was bone tired. The drive home was gentle and almost meditative. I'd held his hand, feeling the soreness between my legs like a reminder of all the good in my life.

We didn't talk about my horrid performance. We didn't talk about the collar. We just sat in peace, and it was perfect.

In front of the bathroom mirror, naked from the waist up, I looked at my collar. It was nice, as collars went. Didn't look doggish. Didn't look slavish. It looked like a really nice piece of jewelry with a lock on the front. The ring in the back was a giveaway though. But the chain mail made it conform to my movements and even, dare I think it, made it comfortable.

"Jonathan?" I called. I could hear him puttering around the bedroom.

"Yeah?"

"Where's the key to this thing?"

"In the box it came in."

"Which is where?"

I didn't even finish the sentence before he was in the bathroom, holding out a black jewelry box. I opened it.

My tuning fork was inside. That wasn't right. I put it on the counter and lifted the velvet panel that the fork rested on. No key hid in the bottom of the box.

"Shit," I said.

"Where was the tuning fork supposed to go?" he asked.

"A little black box. Okay, they got switched. It's around. Let me check my bag."

My phone dinged just as I got there. It was Darren.

—You left a black box with a key in the dressing room. I got it but we're on the flight to Nashville—

I showed Jonathan the phone. "You put the tuning fork away."

"No, you put it in the box."

"And you put the box in your pocket."

"Thinking it was the box with the key."

"And I was responsible for the tuning fork. Goddamnit! I'm so stupid," I said.

"I can have it sawed off your neck."

"Go to hell, Drazen."

He put his hands up as if he was dealing with a crazy person. "I'll have someone fly to Nashville to get the key. I can't have it here by morning, but I can have it off you before Dodger Stadium."

"I'm so mad."

"I know."

"Just free-floating mad."

"I don't want to deflect but—"

"But what?"

"Between your anger, the no-shirt thing, and the collar? You have never looked so fuckable."

My shoulders drooped, and the rage fell right out of me. I held my arms up, and he wrapped himself around me and just hugged me for all it was worth.

chapter fifteen

MONICA

Jonathan's gaze was a continuous companion. He owned me with it. He called his pilot to go to Nashville with his eyes on me. He undressed me slowly by the brightest lamp and made love to me so tenderly it hurt. He touched my neck all the time, drawing his fingers over the bumps in the collar and his thumb over the lock. The next morning, his gaze peeled me open from across the room, and he watched me go out the door as if in a state of utter gratification.

I worried on the way to Mrs. Yuan's that everyone was looking at me with hunger. I felt undressed.

She had a pink hibiscus in her hair. I'd seen them growing outside, and I resisted the urge to touch it to see if it was real.

"Is that going to constrict you?" was the first thing she asked. Not a surprise.

"I don't think so."

She turned to Sherri. "Was she wearing it last night?"

"No, ma'am."

"Well," she said, turning back to me, "from what I understand, we have nowhere to go but up."

My face got hot. Sherri wouldn't look at me even when my eyes burned holes into her.

"It was pretty bad," I said.

"Good," she said, surprising me. "I'd hate for you to peak too soon. And it's out of your system. You survived it. Nothing can hurt you now."

I felt inexplicably relieved, as if she'd given me some sort of indefinable permission I'd been unable to give myself. Not permission to succeed or fail. Permission to just do the thing without calling it a name.

She removed her fork from the box. "Let's start with some scales. Then work on our transition to *banner*."

I tilted my head right then left, feeling the collar bend with me.

"You will be good," she said.

I lowered my lids, as if I had to see her through a narrower opening. Had she said something *nice*? "I'm still not Whitney Houston."

"No, you are not Whitney Houston. You'll do it without changing the phrasing."

She tapped her fork before I could absorb what she'd said, and I hit the note, working back and forth as we'd done for two weeks.

The rehearsal was light and more positive than usual. Mrs. Yuan had more exhortations up her sleeve than I'd given her credit for, and she didn't look at the collar once more. But she and Sherri were the only ones to see me, and I'd made plans to be in public that afternoon to get my mind off the evening.

Once in the car, I checked my texts.

Yvonne:

—*I'll be at Earth in twenty—*

Jonathan:

—Having coordination issues in Nashville. They'll get it here before you sing. Or I'll get a locksmith to break it.—

Well, no. The collar jammed my uncomfortable places, but I had to admit it was nice. I liked it, and I didn't want it broken. He said he'd buy me another, but I didn't want another one. This was the one he'd gotten me, it was the one I wanted, and I wanted it exactly the way he got it.

Whole and with a key.

—I don't think I can make Earth today—

—Bullshit - you show up. Today it's my problems—

—What happened???—

—Men are shit—

I touched the collar. I hadn't been out in public with it. Not really.

Sometimes I was left alone and treated like any other Angeleno, and sometimes the paparazzi showed up. I never knew when I was watched and when I wasn't. I took a deep breath. It was too hot for a scarf or turtleneck. Even if I ran out and got a lightweight neck wrap, covering my collar with it would only announce that I was ashamed. The only thing worse than wearing it in public was broadcasting shame over it.

Fuck it. Yvonne needed me.

chapter sixteen

MONICA

—Lil's driving me to Santa Monica at five. Picking the key up myself – but it's going to be close. I'm sorry—

Santa Monica Airport to Echo Park on a game night, at rush hour, on a Friday, during the school year. Game time was seven. Close didn't begin to cut it.

I'd heard Yvonne out and tried to soothe her. Cursed every penis-owning human in the universe while simultaneously exonerating Jonathan in my head. I hated seeing her in pain and didn't even know what to promise her except my devotion.

On the way out of Earth, I ran into a herd of paparazzi, and what the waiters didn't notice and the patrons ignored, the paps caught immediately.

What's on your neck, Monica?
Is that a lock?
Moooniiiiiicaaaaaaa
Turn so we can see it!

I smiled and waved, trying to keep the pounding of my heart out of my expression. But one girl pap with rings up and down her fingers leaned over my car and got an angle no one else had. The shutter slapped over and over.

Fuck it.

I moved my hair so she got a clear shot of it. *Print that, bitch.*

She moved her camera so I could see her face. "Thank you!" And she disappeared into the crowd.

I got in the car before any of the rest of them could get a clear shot. Because, fuck it. That shot should be worth real money to someone.

The stadium was a short hop away, at least by Friday traffic standards.

But I checked my phone when I parked by the players' entrance, and my collar was all over the gossip pages. How did I feel, seeing what everyone else was seeing? Me pulling my hair away to show off a chain mail locked collar?

I felt like *his.*

It was as if he was standing beside me next to the Jag, holding my hand to make sure nothing bad happened. It was a buffer between the world and me, a shield against people's eyes and intentions. It attracted stares, yes. But in a way, it warded them off. Drained them of their power. Protected me from anything I didn't embrace.

Did it only work in photos? Or—if I changed my attitude—would it work in person?

Only one way to tell.

I twisted up my hair, checking in the rearview for strays, and sang *of the braaaaavvveeeeee* into the mirror.

Sounded good. I was ready to go.

chapter seventeen

Another day. Another dressing room. I worked on my intervals and scales, tuning my voice to a vibrating fork, and checked myself in the mirror. I felt ready. My dress came just below the knee and two inches above the cleavage line, sleeves covering me tight to the elbow. The beads looked dull and lifeless in the flat light of the cinderblock room, but would flash in the stadium lights.

And the collar, well…the collar was another thing entirely.

It made me look like I'd been captured in the wild and brought to heel, and behind a closed door, alone, I liked the idea that I was an animal that needed taming.

Jonathan texted.

—We're on the 110. I'm getting out and running—

—NO! not safe!—

A knock came at the door. I checked my watch. It was go time.

—Freeway's a parking lot. It's safer than crossing La Cienega with the light—

—Please please please be careful.

He didn't answer. Someone knocked again and said. "Two minutes." Gary. The pregame coordinator.

"I got this," I said, smoothing my skirt. "I got this."

***

Last year's Cy Young Award winner stared, absently tossing the ball up and catching it. I felt as if I didn't need a key at that point, because people's eyes were burning a hole in the collar already. Since Jonathan had texted that he was running into traffic to deliver the key, I'd met eight players I admired, including one whose batting stance I wanted to correct every time I watched him at the plate, and the manager, who I wanted to slap over the previous year's play-offs.

"My wife is a huge fan," the pitcher said. "If you sign this, we can trade."

Perfect little athlete smile as he handed me the ball. We were in the cinderblock hallway leading out onto the field. Jonathan hadn't texted since he told me he was running across the 110 with the key to my collar. If he was a grease spot, I would kill him.

The pitcher was looking at my tits. I took the ball, and I gave him the one I'd passed around.

"You gonna pick off Fredricks tonight?" I asked while I wrote my name in Sharpie on the curved surface.

"That's the plan."

"You've got the best pickoff move in the league," I said, handing it back. "If anyone can do it, you can."

He handed me my ball back and looked me in the eye. "Thanks. That's a nice vote of confidence."

"Go get 'em, killer."

Gary, the coordinator of the pregame activities, handed me a mic. "You ready?"

"Yeah."

The umps and managers stood on the mound, talking about I didn't even know what. After they broke and went to their places, the color guard would come out, and that was my cue to go in and sing.

"Wait!" came a breathless voice.

"Jonathan!"

He was huffing and panting down the hall in his dress shoes.

"Are you all right? Your heart!"

He waved away all my concerns. "Please. Easy run." He held up the key, still panting. "But I got here in time."

He was so perfect, chest heaving, broad shoulders back, jaw straight and sharp as he smiled. His green eyes shone with clarity and strength. My gorgeous man, by my side always. We were surrounded by people and not one of them could touch us.

"I'm sorry," I said, putting my hand on his forearm. "You ran…it's got to be half a mile uphill but…"

He tilted his head, waiting.

"Can I keep it on?" I touched the collar reflexively. "I'm sorry. I changed my mind."

He laughed. I'd never heard a sound so right.

"Go," Gary said, guiding me out.

"Go!" Jonathan reiterated.

"Thank you." I kissed his mouth, tasting salt and feeling the scratch of his upper lip.

He put his hands on my cheeks and lengthened the kiss. "Get out of here, goddess. I'm watching."

One quick kiss on his cheek, and I stepped past Gary onto the field. The expanse was bigger than I ever imagined possible, the crowd louder, the pressure more intense. Somewhere in Echo Park, a girl with a voice was listening, and I sang for her, so that when her day came, she wouldn't be afraid.

chapter eighteen

MONICA

Jonathan had sent Lil home and driven me home in my car. I closed my eyes when he pulled down our drive, listening to the cracking of pebbles under the tires and the beating rumble of ocean waves.

The crickets around our house were sand-colored with back legs that bent away from their bodies and to the horizon, not toward the sky. They creaked all seasons of the year, as if they wanted to fuck all the time. When Jonathan opened my door, their mating call filled my ears.

We'd skipped the game. We didn't even have to talk about it. I could see if Fredricks got picked off in tomorrow's news.

I took his hand and let him help me out. The dim spotlights that dotted the curved walkway were the only illumination.

"We should've gotten a place with a porch," he said, lacing his fingers in mine. Only good stuff had happened on his old porch, back when he'd subtly made sure I didn't enter his house with my clothes on.

"I miss your craftsman," I said.

"Me too." He stopped at the front door and gently put his hand around my throat, feeling the collar. "You were magnificent tonight."

"Thank you."

He put the code in the door lock, and it popped open.

"You're not a fraud," he said, moving his hand up to my face. "You're very real."

With the door open and the promise of a night under him a step away, I turned and parted my lips, letting his finger slide between them. I flicked my tongue along the length of it then took it all in my mouth. With a sharp breath, his own lips parted as I cupped my puckered lips around his finger and slid it out.

"My mouth is yours," I said. "I have an idea."

"An idea?"

"I think you'll like it."

***

I was on my back on the kitchen table. Jonathan had made sure the staff was gone for the night, and once that was cleared up, I'd gotten undressed, down to my black garters, and gotten on the hard, flat surface.

"This idea," he said, stroking inside my legs and hooking his finger on the crotch of my panties. "I like it already."

As I pushed myself back until my head hung over the edge of the table, he pulled off my underwear. I let my head drop until I could see through the glass doors to the backyard. The world went upside down. I gripped the sides of the table, so intense was the feeling that I'd fall over.

Jonathan stood beside of me and stroked me from cunt to tits.

"May I have it? Please?" I groaned.

"Have what?"

"Your cock in my mouth. Down my throat. Come down my throat."

He took out his cock. Magnificent beast, dripping with salty pre-come, and he put it to my tongue to lick off.

He put his fingers on my lips. With a sharp inhale, he shoved his fingers into my mouth. I opened my throat, pressing down the back of my tongue. My throat, the collar was exposed to his eyes, and he touched it with his other hand.

"Open. I'm going to fuck your mouth."

I did, and he pushed his fingers down. All the way down. The sinews of my neck pushed against the collar, and he groaned when he pulled them out.

"Take it," he said, putting the tip of his dick to my lips. "Take it all."

I could only feel it. I felt my body, out and vulnerable, his cock invading my throat. I closed my eyes. He pulled out to let me breathe, and I heaved.

"You all right?" he asked.

"Yes, sir." I was still facing upside down, collar exposed to the ceiling. I opened up for him, and he guided his dick back in.

"That collar," he said as he put his length down the throat extended before him. "Fuck. You're mine."

He put his hand between my legs as he fucked my face, timing it again so he had three strokes, then I got a breath. His hand pressed against my cunt, gathering fire. I pushed my hips into him, screaming in pleasure against his cock.

He grunted, pulled out. "Breathe!"

It was a command, an order, and I pulled in a breath before he shoved himself back in, invading me, breaking me, leveraging himself with my tits.

"God," he growled and came in the back of my mouth, marking it.

Sticky in my throat, and salty as he released onto my tongue. Forward again, the last few drops down deep. He released my tits on the last thrust and drew his hands across the collar, pulling on the lock. He gasped and pulled away so I could see him.

"Thank you," he said. "Thank you."

I was too full of him to answer.

I lifted my head to get the blood flow back, and he picked me up. He carried me toward the stairs, but we didn't make it past the living room. He dropped me on the couch and kneeled before me, kissing inside my legs. I ran my fingers through his hair and let his mouth do its work. He didn't let me come but mounted me when he was ready, fucking me until I stiffened and arched, coming with him, breathing deeply to a shared rhythm.

THE END

I have another kinky billionaire lined up for 2016.
Are you ready for Dash Wallace?

Preorder *Kinky Sexy Dirty*

AMAZON - iBOOKS – NOOK

If you're interested seeing where Jonathan and Monica's
scorching journey began:

You can get the bundled versions of
The Submission Series

1) Beg/Tease/Submit
2) Control/Burn/Resist
3) Sing/Coda/Dominance

Or individual novellas

1) Beg
2) Tease
3) Submit
4) Control
5) Burn
6) Resist
7) Sing
8) Dominance (A Submission Reader)
9) Coda

If you want to know more about what it's like to sing at a baseball game, or even why the "Star-Spangled Banner" is the most sadistic song in the world, check out Drew Magary's retelling of his experience.

http://deadspin.com/5928720/whats-it-like-to-sing-the-anthem-at-a-baseball-game-the-story-of-one-mans-perilous-fight

www.ingramcontent.com/pod-product-compliance
Lightning Source LLC
Chambersburg PA
CBHW061500210726
48287CB00007B/2596